Selvakumar Knew Better

Written by Virginia Kroll
Illustrated by Xiaojun Li

Library of Congress Cataloging-in-Publication Data

Kroll, Virginia L.
  Selvakumar knew better / by Virginia Kroll ; illustrated by Xiaojun
Li.
      p. cm.
  Summary: When a giant tsunami approaches his village, seven-year-old
Dinakaran is saved by the family dog. Based on a true story; includes
facts about the 2004 Indian Ocean tsunami.
  ISBN-13: 978-1-885008-29-9
  ISBN-10: 1-885008-29-5
  [1. Indian Ocean Tsunami, 2004--Fiction. 2. Tsunamis--Fiction. 3.
Dogs--Fiction. 4. India--Fiction.] I. Li, Xiaojun, ill. II. Title.

PZ7.K9227.Sel 2006
[E]--dc22

2006002183

Printed in China

Book design and production by Patty Arnold, Menagerie Design and Publishing www.menageriedesign.net

For Daisy, Yin-Yang, and Bella,
my current canine companions. — V.K.

In memory of my brother Huaixiao — X.L.

The December day in south India dawned like any other, kissed by the golden sun. Papa came back with his boat full of fish. Mama made breakfast for seven-year-old Dinakaran and his two little brothers. That day seemed like any other day, but Selvakumar knew better.

He paced and felt a rumbling in his belly. His legs were restless, and his scruffy yellow fur stood on end. His ears perked up, listening for the sound that had already started.

His family didn't notice. Papa was busy unloading his catch. Mama was hanging her laundry. Dinakaran was sitting in the shade, finishing his homework, while the younger boys chased each other around the yard.

Selvakumar whined, and Mama said, "Hush." Selvakumar barked, and Dinakaran complained, "Quiet, I'm trying to concentrate."

Suddenly, a strange roaring sound began. Mama half-heard, thinking that a thunderstorm was coming and wondering whether she should stop hanging the wash. Dinakaran and his brothers thought it was an extra-loud train. Papa said, "Is that a supersonic jet about to crash into the sea?" and ran to a nearby building's roof to investigate.

But Selvakumar knew better. The vibrations traveled up his padded paws. His skin prickled with fearful goosebumps from his black nose to his tufted tail. He wanted to run, but he dared not leave his family. Sometimes humans didn't realize.

Why were they waiting? Didn't they know that a mighty earthquake had rumbled under the ocean and would soon bring raging waves onto the shore?

And then Papa shouted from the rooftop, "Tsunami! Run!" in a tone he'd never used before.

Mama instantly dropped the clothes. "Sons, come on!" she ordered. She grabbed a little one under each arm and screamed, "Dinakaran, run! You're swift and strong. Follow me. Up the hill. Fast as you can!"

But the roar had gotten louder, cutting off her words. All that Dinakaran had heard was, "Run!" And run he did, back to his family's small square house, forty yards from the shore.

"Home," he panted, huddling in a corner. "I'll be safe here."

But Selvakumar knew better. He barked and howled, but Dinakaran couldn't hear him. The sound of the approaching waves drowned his voice out, too.

Selvakumar nipped at Dinakaran's heels, but the boy wouldn't budge. "Go." Dinakaran shooed the dog away, but Selvakumar knew better, and would not give up. He grabbed Dinakaran's shirt in his teeth. He jerked and pulled and tugged until his teeth hurt. With all his strength, he dragged Dinakaran back outside and bumped him from behind. Finally the boy understood.

Selvakumar took off toward the hill, looking back to make sure Dinakaran was following. "Yep!" he yelped, and he and Dinakaran raced uphill as the enormous wall of water chased them. The tsunami roared louder than five thunderstorms, ten trains, and twenty supersonic jets put together.

Selvakumar and Dinakaran didn't stop running until they reached the upper road. Their sides ached and they panted heavily, their breaths feeling like hot coals burning in their chests. Dinakaran wanted to stop, but Selvakumar knew better. He nudged Dinakaran's hand, and together they continued higher up the hill.

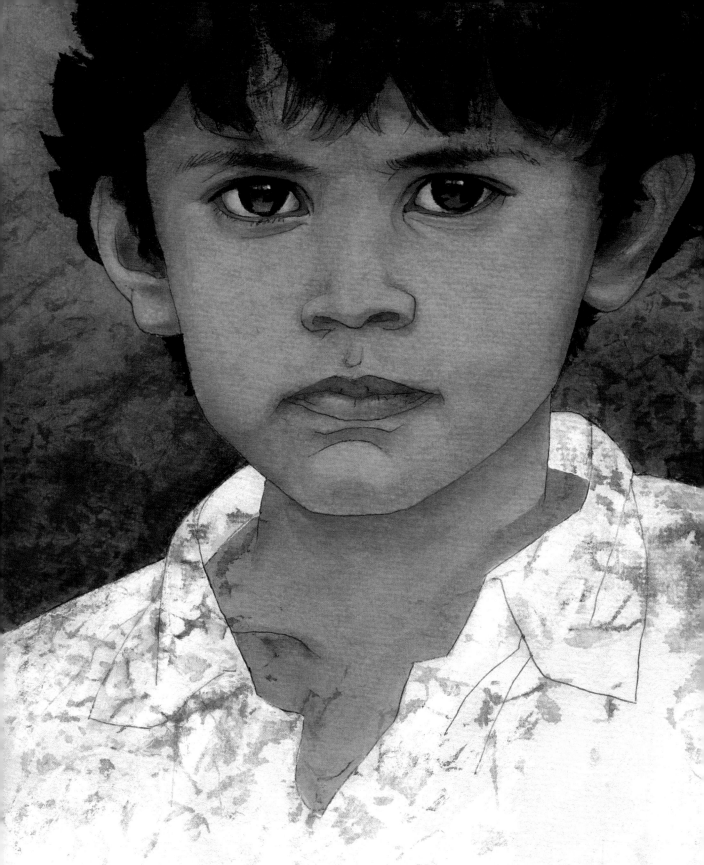

Finally, they turned and looked down toward the shore.
Selvakumar nuzzled against Dinakaran's knee, and
they both blinked their dark brown eyes in disbelief.

The wave had swallowed
Mama's wash and
Papa's catch. It had
snapped trees as if they
were brittle little sticks
and collapsed all the
houses flat as if they'd
been stork nests of
loose straw.

In the distance, Selvakumar and Dinakaran heard Mama's voice. "Dinakaran," she wailed over and over. "My firstborn son is lost!" They walked toward the sound and found her rocking back and forth as her younger sons sobbed beside her.

Selvakumar yipped and bounded toward her. Mama's head snapped up. She swiped her tears and stared at Dinakaran. "My precious son, you're alive!" she whispered. Dinakaran rushed into her arms, and she covered him in grateful kisses.

"I-I went to th-the house, Mama. I-I thought I'd be sa-safe. B-but Sel-Selvakumar knew better," he sputtered as his own tears mixed with Mama's fresh ones. He told her about what the dog had done.

Mama let go of Dinakaran and hugged Selvakumar until he thought that she might smother him. He wriggled free and greeted the smaller boys with face-licks and body-wrestles.

Papa joined them after the tsunami disappeared, and when he heard the story, he sobbed into Selvakumar's fur, too. Then they were all a mother-father-brothers-dog thankful heap of hugging.